Sing a Song of Piglets

Sing a Song of Piglets

A Calendar in Verse

by

EVE BUNTING

Pictures by

EMILY ARNOLD MCCULLY

Clarion Books
New York

Clarion Books
a Houghton Mifflin Company imprint
215 Park Avenue South, New York, NY 10003
Text copyright © 2002 by Eve Bunting
Illustrations copyright © 2002 by Emily Arnold McCully

The illustrations were executed in watercolor.
The text was set in 18-point Garamond.
Book design by Janet Pedersen.

www.houghtonmifflinbooks.com

Printed in Singapore

Library of Congress Cataloging-in-Publication Data

Bunting, Eve, 1928–
Sing a song of piglets / by Eve Bunting ; illustrated by Emily Arnold McCully.
p. cm.
Summary: From skiing in January to surfing in July, two energetic piglets romp through the months of the year in this calendar in verse.
ISBN 0-618-01137-4
1. Children's poetry, American. 2. Piglets—Juvenile poetry. 3. Months—Juvenile poetry. [1. Pigs—Poetry. 2. Months—Poetry.
3. American poetry.] I. McCully, Emily Arnold, ill. II. Title.
PS3552.U4735 S56 2002
811'.54—dc21   2001055267

TWP   10 9 8 7 6 5 4 3 2 1

1266

For James Cross Giblin
—E.B.

January

Sing a song of skiing,
skiing in the snow.
Wax your skis
and bend your knees
and down the hill we go.

February

Sing a song of skating,
skating on the ice.
Skim and slide
and swoop and glide.
Pigs on ice look nice!

March

Sing a song of shamrocks,
tucked behind each ear.
A scarf that's green,
a tambourine . . .
St. Patrick's Day is here.

April

Sing a song of gardening,
digging with a hoe.
Pull the weeds
and plant the seeds
and watch the flowers grow.

13

Sing a song of fishing,
fishing in the bay.
Cast your line,
we're doing fine.
Oh! That one got away.

Sing a song of softball,
standing at the plate.
I got a hit!
I clobbered it!
Time to celebrate!

July

Sing a song of surfing,
surfing in the sea.
Hang your toes,
the whole world knows
we're fearless as can be.

19

August

Sing a song of reading,
lying in the shade.
Chapter Three,
you read to me!
And pass the lemonade.

20

Sing a song of falling leaves,
covering the ground.
Scatter them
and splatter them
and toss them all around.

October

Sing a song of dressing up
in a great disguise.
He's a bat
and I'm a cat
with super scary eyes.

24

November

Sing a song of feasting,
everything's a treat.
Hash and mash,
potato smash.
Piglets love to eat.

27

December

Sing a song of giving,
gifts beneath the tree.
A music box,
bright woolen socks,
and bikes for you and me.

Sing a song of seasons,
lots of things to do.
They would be fun
with only one . . .

. . . but I'm so glad we're two!